A GIFT FOR MISS MILO

A Gift for Miss Milo

by Jan Wahl

Illustrated by Jeff Grove

JF WAH

Wahl, Jan.

A Gift for Miss Milo

TEN SPEED PRESS
Berkeley, California

1☺
TEN SPEED PRESS
P O Box 7123
Berkeley, California 94707

Cover design by Nancy Austin
Text design by Faith and Folly
Typeset in Stone Serif

Library of Congress Cataloging-in-Publication Data

Wahl, Jan.
    A gift for Miss Milo / by Jan Wahl ; illustrated by Jeff Grove.
        p.   cm.
    Summary: An old woman waits for the man who would have been
    her bridegroom if he hadn't vanished into another dimension.
        ISBN 0-89815-329-8
        [1. Mountain life—Fiction.]   I. Grove, Jeff, ill. II. Title.
    PZ7.W1266Gi   1989
    [Fic]—dc20   90-33237
                                                                CIP
                                                                 AC

Printed in the United States of America

1   2   3   4   5   —   94   93   92   91   90

For my Weronika

It's me, Mattie Sprunk. I am carrying Miss Milo's sheets in my arm. I take them to her house two times a year.

Once in winter, as I am doing now.

And once in summer. They are for her special bed which she never slept in.

Miss Milo's house is set off far from the road like all large farm houses near here. It is painted strong yellow. Mr. Hirem still paints it, although she died almost four years ago. In her will she gave money for that, saying the house must be bright in color.

So that Charley Fender will be able to find it. Charley went off into another dimension she said, and will pop back the same young age as when he left. Maybe he'll find his way back today.

I wish he would. He might be able to explain a lot of things. Now I don't mind coming out here by myself. I like to ride my bicycle into the deep of the country. We live at the edge of town. Our town is Oriole Springs, a dumb name but I can't help it.

I like walking across thick, bushy grass on her lawn. Most of all, I like going inside her empty house.

On Hallowe'en nobody breaks windows here. Charley Fender might step from a lost dimension and grab you.

Maybe a lot of things. People just stay away. My father says I am not like other girls he knows, for they wouldn't take my place if a box of diamonds were placed inside the great yellow house I'm walking toward.

Really, I missed the first meeting of our Knicker-bocker Twinkies just to come. Edna Hubbs and Mary Alice Kerbawy said I must be as crazy as Miss Milo was to do it. That's because they weren't acquainted with Miss Milo.

My grandmother was her best friend. I think the only friend she had. My grandmother often let me come with her when she used to visit.

And it's because of Charley Fender I put clean, freshly ironed sheets on a beautiful poster bed. I helped my mother iron them this morning. We took great care with them, since they are of costly Irish linen and have designs stitched in the border.

You see, Charley, the one who vanished into another dimension, was going to marry Miss Milo. Reverend Riggle was there and everything. This is a fact.

I know some other facts from the Oriole Register. One at a time, though.

Miss Milo once took me to the very place where Charley passed into another dimension on that day long ago. It's in a huge weedy hollow that nobody ever filled in next to the old country schoolhouse beside the Milo property.

We have a lot of abandoned spots, since people go to the city to live and nobody cares. I care. Miss Milo took me to the spot and declared *this* is where she heard him, moaning. His ankle hurt, he told her. He had tumbled into another dimension and was awfully hungry.

She was hunting for him for days of course and sat on a log trying to think what to do. She hurried back to her home and put some nice fried chicken in a lunch bucket, and she sat on an oak log and talked to him for hours.

He couldn't reach the bucket right away. Sometimes his voice faded off and often was clear as a bell. Well, she described it so. It grew chilly in the evening

. . . the very place where Charley passed into another dimension . . .

and Charley urged her to get back to the home they almost shared.

And she did and here is the fact part: in the morning, when Miss Milo ran to the hollow where he was, the fried chicken was gone. Now what kind of animal is it that can unhitch the hinge on a lunch bucket and close it up again?

No kind, that's who, and Charley's spirits were better and he was hopeful of getting back. He instructed her to pull and she did.

It was no use, she couldn't get hold of him and before she could return with more help Charley had faded off into nowhere.

Some folks in town say Charley Fender ran away to become a pipe fitter for the Clover Leaf Railway.

If you weren't there, you just have to pick and choose what seems best, then. That is my philosophy. Mine, Mattie Sprunk's.

My grandmother never admits believing this about Charley falling off into the void. My grandmother is a practical person. But she always defends Miss Milo, her friend, if people gossip and declare Miss Milo was surely touched in the head.

Love and growing old, in general, are strange ways to me. I don't truly understand them yet. Though probably I will soon in a few years.

It has been partly through Miss Milo that I have found out about these things. I don't mean I found out by any words she spoke to me. She said very little. But I have heard people in town talk of her and her story—and I have watched.

Watched her, I mean. This has all made Love a mystery to us. Even to Genevive Bistline, the homeliest girl in school.

And I am willing for it to happen to me. There are so many clews. A person, some day, has to fit them together in a wonderful fashion, I guess.

Love puzzles me just as Miss Milo's story does.

When I am looking at the house like I'm looking now, it seems true, like they say. The house *does* sag on the end near the two maple trees.

For the house is furnished only at that end. Miss Milo never bothered to put furniture in the rooms

on the other side of the house, since she lived by herself and needed no more than what she herself could use.

There is a kitchen with a hand pump that's painted with gold-looking paint. And a sitting room as they called it in Miss Milo's day. And another, and smaller, sitting room upstairs. And also the bedroom.

They are very beautiful. Nearly every stick of furniture in them, and every drapery too, was sent away for. Chosen with much care.

Sometimes I walk through the empty rooms and partly close my eyes and think of how they would have looked. Except for the bedroom, everything is gone, sold by my grandmother for taxes and upkeep.

In Miss Milo's day they had brightly colored oil paintings. In almost every corner there was a music box or piano or pump organ or cage of canaries. For Miss Milo liked all kinds of colors (some of the windows have bits of peculiar glass in them) and she liked music.

Music it is said brought Lavesta Margaret Milo and Charley Fender together. Handsome young Charley sang tenor in The Ice House Quartet. If ever this group sang at a social, soon Miss L. M. Milo's good white gloves were heard. Clapping loudly.

My uncle Mike Fruth hints *maybe* much traveling up and down the County for many concerts once gave Charley an itch to travel. To think far beyond Oriole Springs.

I'll never forget once my grandmother and I paid Miss Milo a visit. It was evening and the three of us drifted creaking softly on her porch swing.

Only two hooks are left in the ceiling.

Suddenly Miss Milo went inside and sat down in the dark to play the upright piano.

She played from Ethelbert Nevins' "A Day in Venice" suite and the porch swing swayed like a gondola. At least it seemed to, while she played. I've

tried learning this piece yet I do not have the knack.
Not like Miss Milo!

Later, we were in the kitchen, drinking lemonade.
She told us whenever she played she wanted Charley
Fender to hear and to be able to follow it to where he
heard the sounds coming from.

If only he would sing out and join us! Miss Milo
usually spoke of Charley Fender as though he were
very NEAR.

Almost near enough to be called. Just as if he were
a little beyond Morgan's Hill. Or on the other side of
Pike Creek. Or somewhere in the middle of her own
orchard.

Sometimes, she seemed to forget she had told me
about his stumbling into the void.

I mean in that place in a weedy hollow.

Lots of queer things happen to make me wonder. But are never truly explained. No, not like my body is now changing. I've been with Vianna Eicholtz and Lucy Trapp behind the Trapp garage, questioning that. I suppose if I stayed for the meeting of the Knickerbocker Twinkies I would know more.

Something more mysterious is what I mean. Like when I was a child:

I was standing near the canning factory and looking across the fields next to it. And I saw a cloud of pink smoke twisting, rolling up into the air.

It wasn't an explosion. There came no noise. And no fire was reported in our newspaper. I've never again seen smoke like this.

It was the same color as the lemonade Miss Milo colored by spooning a few drops of cherry juice in it. I never discovered where the smoke was, or who made it.

Also, I do not understand to this day just WHY Charley Fender ran away and never married Miss Milo. Or if she made up that story about his dipping into another dimension.

Anyhow most people say he ran off. On their wedding day. My father guesses Charley probably already had a wife. Someone he met on tour with

And I saw a cloud of pink smoke . . .

that Ice House Quartet. So he moved into another state farther west. Uncle Mike says he wasn't the kind to get married even though he loved Miss Milo.

He declares Charley was forced into proposing after the law case. I will tell you about it in a minute.

Miss Milo herself never admitted she knew the reason.

Instead, she was always sure Charley Fender would return at any moment. That perhaps on their wedding day he walked in the wrong direction and would discover, sooner or later, he made a mistake? I don't know. No one could argue that he had disappeared.

In the daytime, Miss Milo, when I knew her, sat in the upper hallway at the large front window, looking across buckwheat and corn and alfalfa fields, across Pike Creek too, to Morgan's Hill where wild mustard grows.

She was determined it was most likely he would appear there first. So she faced in that direction.

She was always dressed up and waiting to go out and get married the moment he came back into the house he'd built for her. Sometimes I think she wore her best clothes even as she slept, since he might just as well come in during the night.

Maybe that abandoned schoolhouse bell would begin to clang?

Perhaps Miss Milo was old. I can't tell exactly.

She was raised in a time of horse and buggy and still owned a horse when our town was full of automobiles. A chore she did faithfully was curry Tamerzon and clean his stall.

Folks whispered she rode him at midnight searching for Charley but I don't believe it. Did she do that?

I remember standing next to her dressing table. My grandmother carefully arranged her hair. Miss Milo did not use electricity. Candles were lit.

Their dim light hid her wrinkles. They shone about Miss Milo's face and on faded wallpaper. She put make-up on thickly. I guess she didn't know it, for her eyes were used to staring far across fields and she couldn't see well up close.

She told us it was important for her to stay beautiful since Charley Fender would expect it. Charley, I guess, was going to stay fresh as a daisy.

We helped her put on, over a corset, a silk embroidered dress that came by boat from Hungary. Fine lace was sewn at the wrists and neck. Miss Milo carried a white bonnet, holding the loops of it in her left hand. When we walked downstairs I couldn't help noticing the sparkling engagement ring.

Often she rubbed it, making sure it was still there.

You can snicker at her as my friends did but I can't.

That night she stood at the bottom of the stairs and turned to Grandmother and me. She said that she was holding her white imported bonnet because a wind was starting to blow then and she'd have need of a hat in case Charley Fender came to take her away that same night.

Grandmother kept silent. I noticed she bit her tongue. Already Miss Milo had shown us the great leather trunk packed and waiting in her closet.

I've examined the clothes inside many times. It's like watching a queen's wardrobe with silks and velvets and satins brought from far countries. Stitched in the corner of her clothes was her name: LAVESTA.

Only my grandmother called her that.

To the rest of us she was Miss Milo.

Here is another fact: my grandmother *saw* Miss Milo and Charley Fender walking along the river bank. Often!

There was never another couple like them, she said—smiling in a way that made me see them reflected in the small part of her crinkly eyes.

Miss Milo would be young, with curls tucked tightly into her bonnet.

There would be a long ribbon at her throat floating behind her when she ran—when Charley Fender had to catch up.

She rustled her skirts and flew lightly beside the river bank. Charley Fender, slim and brown-haired, went swiftly like wild deer that lived near the river and in Spicer's Woods in those days.

They would stop then. Sitting together laughing. They would speak of their marriage and the large house they were building.

This is the scene my grandmother watched while she headed to town in those days. Or she might have been strolling with my grandfather. Courting.

That is what they used to do.

Now that area is filled with fishing shanties and a trash dump, the litter from town. Yet I can see what *was* from blue shadows of Grandmother's eyes. And I see it even now, in my mind, crossing Miss Milo's lawn.

I don't care if I missed the first meeting of the Knickerbockers!

I was used to seeing Miss Milo sitting patiently in her stiff chair upstairs. Or rocking back and forth on her porch. Playing the piano. Or doing chores.

But I can imagine what she used to look like when she was young. It's easy to pretend I see things like that—as easy as it is to pull the paper off white birch trees in late summer.

Several of Miss Milo's neighbors did her planting and threshing. They didn't ask any money for it, though she had an ample amount. She was given money by her parents and by Charley Fender's parents.

You see, each was an only child. I suppose it was hoped Charley would settle down. Only my grandmother knows which parents built the house. His? Hers? Maybe both?

Miss Milo rarely ventured into town at the end. However, one afternoon I caught sight of her going down Perry Street.

. . . my grandmother saw Miss Milo and Charley Fender
walking along the river bank.

She'd come to sell sacks of clover seed since she had to give up giving music lessons. It was too far out into the country, after school, for most students.

Sometimes she liked to go a while to the train station, watching the Eastbound or Westbound B & O. There is something wonderful about the moaning whistle of an arriving train engine.

Labeled boxes arrived. Odd, dusty trunks too. The station platform was busy, and she would peer at each visitor.

Without luck. Sometimes she checked with Ilo Gackel of the Oriole Register in case they got news. She hated to do this, said Grandmother. Because of the article that was printed after the law case.

But on this afternoon she stared hard straight ahead like a ship's captain. Not once turning either right or left. It was as if she didn't want to be tempted to linger in town for any reason. But wanted to hurry back to her house in her horse and rig as soon as she took care of her affairs.

She had to stop at Horn's Grocery and that is where I met her. Mr. Horn, like many people in our town, didn't know how to speak with her.

When Horn came around the other side of the counter, bending over a flour barrel (flour clung to

his glasses, clouding them up), I heard her ask if Charley Fender had come by. Just as if she was asking about Reverend Riggle—or Uncle Mike—who passed by, to and fro, any time of day.

Sometimes she felt Charley Fender would come through town first, when he returned. Out of his lost dimension.

Anyhow, Mr. Horn, chewing his black cigar, shook his head briefly from side to side. I think he wanted to pat her hand and apologize for not having glimpsed poor Charley.

But instead he carried out the barrel and said nothing except to remark on the dry spell we were having. Miss Milo appeared to be studying a spider's web.

Suddenly she announced she preferred it dry. She didn't like to think of Charley Fender walking here in a driving rain, she said. I don't know if she really recognized me. But Tamerzon appreciated several cubes of sugar I had stolen from Horn's.

I waved as she left although Vianna Eicholtz and Lucy Trapp were sticking out their tongues at me. I was proud to know her. There was no one else like Miss Milo.

Just why she supposed he'd arrive by FOOT, nobody is certain. It is true that to this day no one knows how he left if he did not fall into that void. He must have walked away or hitched a ride.

Somehow.

When his parents got asked they always said Charley ate a big, hearty breakfast the morning of his wedding. He spoke of his bride-to-be and mentioned how beautiful she was.

Next, he went out in back to fetch rain water to wash in, cutting off a yellow daisy growing in the yard. And handed the daisy to his mother, watching shiny water spill out of the petals. He said he wished Miss Milo (he called her Lavesta) to pin it on at Church.

He rushed upstairs to put on his suit. After Charley got ready, he never was so handsome as *then*. Striding through the room out the front door.

When his mother would describe this, she had to flop in the nearest chair. He said he would take a last look at his home for a minute or two.

There was not another noise heard. Not even a whistle! Nor was as much as his shadow ever seen rounding a corner of the barn or hen house.

Of course the well was examined. But he was not down there.

Since he did not return, his parents decided he'd walked on to Church. So the Fenders went on without him. Everyone sat in Church the rest of the morning until Noon. Fidgeting, worrying.

A bunch of boys who came to hoot and holler and throw rice were asked to find the groom. Charley always showed up for the Ice House Quartet!

My grandmother was maid of honor and remembers this better than her own wedding. My grandpop winks.

Then, Miss Milo, with yellow daisy pinned on, stood up. Her white veil over her face. Otto Mominee the organist had been practicing obbligatos and he squeaked to a stop.

She said the bouquet should be kept by my grand-mother. All might as well go home. No one made a move, however. Because of the veil, it was as if she spoke without moving her lips.

The bridesmaids, who had worked long hours fixing their outfits, started to cry.

Miss Milo had to spend an hour calming *them*. She stayed to make sure the wedding audience ate up special food laid out on wicker tables on the lawn and Otto Mominee played music quietly. What was left of the Ice House Quartet sang a few favorites.

The wedding guests scurried about. Chickens with their heads cut off. And Miss Milo directed every-thing still wearing the veil.

Charley Fender was always light on his feet and left no shoe prints. Perhaps this is why Miss Milo had the idea for his falling into the void?

Anyway—

She decided to move into her "gift" house that same day though only part was finished. She kept all the lights on, waiting for Charley. Somebody who'd gone past in the middle of night said she was playing the piano and singing just like nothing happened.

She wore her wedding dress a full week and told Reverend Riggle (who was young, too) to be ready to marry them. But after a week passed and Charley Fender had not yet returned from his other dimension, she started wearing colored dresses—going-away dresses.

The leather trunk was kept waiting by the front door.

Later on she moved it into the bedroom closet. And that is where the trunk remained.

My grandmother says the thing we must remember Miss Milo for—more than anything else—is her refusing to fade her hopes during all those years.

Grandmother declares her friend wasn't crazy as most people claim. Miss Milo wasn't angry about what happened in her life. Anybody would have known that by looking closely into her eyes like I have done. The eager part of her shone through there, the good, the patient.

. . . she started wearing colored dresses—going-away dresses.

Grandmother says that we *need* somebody like her friend to show us how to wait. Isn't that funny?

Now it may be true Charley stumbled into a void. He might have been kidnapped. Or just as likely he fell into Pike Creek and got drowned. I think about it if I see our country boys fishing with long bamboo poles on summer days when they don't have to help their fathers.

Or maybe it's true what my father or Uncle Mike suggested? Really he already had a wife somewhere else.

And went to where she was. Or he wasn't the kind to get married at all and so he ran off.

Anyhow, Miss Milo chose to believe the rest of her life that whatever had delayed Charley would end and he'd come back.

After a while, she was able to step outdoors to spend part of her days. She grew sunflowers, China roses, and dahlias, flowers that are lasting as well as bright in color. Often she wore a silk apron over a fine dress for traveling.

She'd walk among the flowers, bending over them—trimming—watering. Miss Milo had a green thumb, surely!

Then she had a large duck pond dug. There she raised geese sent in big crates from Australia and special green-and-yellow ducks with bright red button eyes. The ducks came from Singapore.

They are gone now.

Do you suppose Miss Milo imagined if Charley had run off to join a ship he might see her name on the wood crates? I don't know.

Inside the house, if she wasn't sitting upstairs staring out the center window, she would wind up her music boxes. Or play the piano. Or merely listen to songs of imported canaries.

I still hear Miss Milo calling out for me to close the door, quickly, whenever I go into that house.

Because she didn't often keep things caged up! That's why geese and ducks wandered over every inch of her yard. She let the canaries fly about the house if they wished. She trained them to perch on chair-backs or sit on the edge of the table for company.

Singing birds followed her *everywhere*. Oh, Miss Milo!

The reason I wear these hunting boots is because of the mice. It is a house of rodents and cobwebs. But it was not when Miss Milo was here for she was a powerful housekeeper. In fact, in my new boots it is slippery since the floor was oiled.

If Charley returned, he could have seen his face reflected anywhere!

But when she died, we did not find a single mop or dustrag! How do you explain it?

She liked to stop salesmen passing through town. Carefully she described Charley Fender but never

acted defeated when they shook their heads *No* like Horn the Grocer.

She died on a summer's day when men were cutting down corn in her fields. It was fertile soil.

On that afternoon she appeared in the yard wearing one of her best dresses. They said she walked right to the tall metal windmill and climbed up the wire ladder to the top.

They thought she was about to jump! No, she scanned the horizon as hard as she could. Seeing more of the world, I think, than she'd ever caught sight of before. Then she went back inside and before the day was out she was "gone."

Miss Milo never slept in the poster bed in the bedroom. Instead, she always went to sleep on a horse hair sofa in the small sitting room.

Curling up like a cat, she could get into it. That is how my grandmother found her, lying down, all dressed to meet Charley.

My grandmother held a tiny feather under her nose. One of her favorite canaries was perched on her stomach and was silent.

Miss Milo and Charley Fender pop into my head out of nowhere. Even when I'm doing things using my arms and legs and the rest of me.

. . . she walked right to the tall metal windmill and
climbed up the wire ladder to the top.

Last summer I remember I was playing tennis with Mary Alice Kerbawy in the park next to the Waterworks. Mary Alice was jumping and yelling on the other side of the net, making lots of noise.

I thought of them, missing my serve!

They were strolling along the river, lingering a while by it. Early morning mist was rising. Both could spy tiny floating moss islands on the water's surface.

They walked past a row of bushes that looked like green, lacy sponges. The long red ribbon at Miss Milo's neck was trailing down her back.

Mary Alice's thumping on the hard clay court is sort of silly.

Don't you think?

Miss Milo puzzles me so. Why didn't SHE leave also? My great-grandparents drove to Oriole Springs in covered wagons drawn by mules. Three weeks on the way from Muncie, Pennsylvania.

They set up a log cabin chinked and dabbed with mud. Why did some folks come from so far to here? Why do some leave? Why do others stay? Where is it I will find *my* life?

Here is part of the story I left out since it is the strangest part.

It's about the law case. One time, Miss Milo had not one "caller" but two. Who can *ever* understand grown-ups?

I am not making this up because IT IS A FACT. The other fellow became a successful farmer at Liberty Bend. His name was Clarence McGill. He died long ago.

I begged my uncle Mike to tell me this wasn't so and I went one day to ask him at the Oriole Register, where he is typesetter. We looked it up in a musty bound volume of years ago.

They called it "sparking," chuckled Uncle Mike. The newspaper was yellowed. He believes the case occurred because Miss Milo had an interest in Charley Fender but this Clarence McGill had his eye on her also.

Perhaps she egged Clarence on so Charley would make up his mind? Well, when Uncle Mike's back was turned I tore out the page and I can tell you the report by memory!

✓ORIOLE REGISTER

THIRTY-SIXTH YEAR   "ONLY the TRUTH"   PRICE IN ORIOLE COUNTY 1 CENT OUTSIDE 2 CENT

SEE TOMORROW'S REGISTER FOR BARGAIN GUIDE

There came off today before Police Justice Hubbard, in this township, a singular lawsuit, growing out of the following particulars: Charles W. Fender and Clarence Z. McGill, two young men about twenty-five years of age, have for some months been courting a young lady.

The men grew jealous of each other and each strove to win the girl's consent to a marriage. But she could not decide which to have. Sunday night of last week the two men were sitting on the porch talking with the girl, when a dispute arose between them as to which was the shortest route to Wauseon, Fender saying by the depot, McGill claiming by the wagon road. They referred the matter to the girl, who laughingly replied that the best way to decide was to walk there and back, each by his route; when they could decide which was the quickest, and as there was but little difference in the distance, she could know which was the smartest man. And, she playfully added, 'Go, noble nights (sic) and he who first returns shall claim my hand in marriage!'

Each man started, Fender disappearing around the corner by the depot route, McGill around the other corner, to go by the wagon road. When McGill returned after a forty minute walk on the hot night he was made still hotter by seeing Fender coolly sitting on the porch where he had been for thirty-five minutes, as he only stepped around the corner and returned, preferring sitting with the young lady to walking three miles over railroad ties.

After some hard words McGill told the girl to go to—, a hotter place than Wauseon, and left the house. He brought suit against the girl to recover pay for the following bill of goods which he had presented her while sparking her. We copy the bill from the Court Records: One gold ring, $5.00; One fancy fan, $3.00; One pair white kids, $3.00; One box confectionery, $2.50, Total $13.50.

On the trial, Hon. Angus Cameron appeared for the prosecution and Brick Pomeroy, by particular request, for the defence (sic) under whose instructions the young lady presented a bill as follows: To kerosene oil, 7 months, $3.00; To rent of parlor for sparking, $10.50; To confectionery eaten by plaintiff, $0.25. Total $13.75.

After a rather amusing trial, during which the plaintiff admitted that he ate of the confectionery he bought the girl, the court gave a verdict of twenty-five cents and costs against the plaintiff. His Honor, Mayor Levy, Judge Flint, Gen. Washburn, ex-mayor Lloyd, and several of our prominent business men were in attendance out of curiosity, and were summoned as witnesses on the part of the defence (sic) as to cost of kerosene, worth of room for sparking purposes, etc., etc. The cost of the suit amounted to $13.62½.

At least Miss Milo laughed once.

Now it's winter's end. I'm carrying the sheets for the poster bed. Miss Milo said in her will the bed should be ready at all times for him in case he has need of it. I bring clean sheets twice a year. Fifty dollars is put in the bank on my birthday by her lawyer, Mr. Dewlap.

Yet it's not like winter this morning.

Sometimes now and then the seasons seem to get mixed up. During the middle of the snow suddenly

. . . the best way to decide was to walk there
and back, each by his own route . . .

the ice and all melt partly away. And I see brown leaves and empty branches left over from fall.

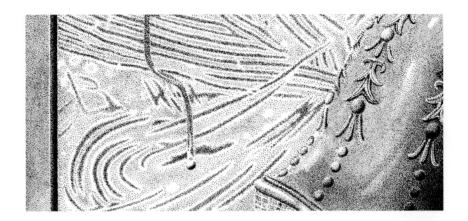

Or sometimes bits of spring come ahead a little. Like when I look closely at a frosted window and I see a clear drop of water running down it, making a warmer path.

Or when I feel a cold breeze on a summer's night, when a small wind has chased it up from the bottom of the creek and turned it toward my open window.

When I notice the seasons getting mixed up like that, it reminds me that soon my life, too, won't be orderly.

When my mother hints at what will come—all the changes—I think that even Miss Milo started out like this. She was like me, once!

She went to parties then. Had to get new dresses. Meet boys. And ask her mother questions.

Will I end up like her? All stuck away in a house?

Today, I know, the Knickerbocker Twinkies are discussing events to be sponsored by Alpha Beta Sorority: there's a Leap Year Dance this week. And a big Maypole Dance on May first. Now later on will be the "Rustic Ramble." Will the older girls let us come? Peewee Bockerman wants to ask me.

After the dance are big ice cream sodas at the Quail's Nest in town.

It is confusing. I suppose I'm not old enough to know if the love of a girl who wore an imported bonnet and who once went walking with a brown-haired boy was worth the waiting!

Particularly if she had to sit in a stiff wooden chair with just a small cushion.

Had Miss Milo played tennis, for instance?

I don't think I'd like to give *that* up.

Today spring has come ahead a bit.

The grass is almost green. Loud bluejays who stay the whole year (I wonder sometimes why they don't like to leave) whistle near me.

The sun is beginning to warm up.

However, tomorrow it'll probably snow again so Pike Creek will be frozen over with ice.

After I put the fresh-smelling sheets on the bed and have dusted here and there, I'll walk through every room of the yellow house. Even the empty ones. I hope the mice will be gone but of course I have my hunting boots on. Then I'll go to the upper hallway and sit for a while in the chair by a large center window that has pieces of bright-colored glass in it.

All right, here I am, in the chair.

Almost every time I come I do this.

I love to see how long I can sit watching over fields and hills. Especially across to the hill where mustard plants grow in the spring.

I wonder about what I've heard.

Sometimes I am positive that in the next minute I'll see Charley Fender racing down the hill out of the void.

Making a wide leap across the creek.

If that happens, I'm glad Mr. Hirem keeps the house painted bright. I'm glad the poster bed is newly made up. And I guess I'll run downstairs to let Charley Fender in.

For—having come such a long, long way—he'll be tired.

A NOTE ON THE ART

The illustrations for *A Gift for Miss Milo* were created by the artist using a method called *pointillism*. Layers of dots were built up to attain the different hues and textures. For example, in the color illustrations: First a layer of blue dots were applied, then a coating of clear acrylic followed by a layer of pink dots, and another coat of clear acrylic. Color after color was applied between coats of acrylic until the entire palette for that specific illustration was used. In order to obtain the fine dots, technical pens with triple-zero points were used on a smooth finish bristol paper. For even smaller dots, the artist encouraged the eventual clogging of the pen, and the restricted flow made the tiny dots possible. Although the artist does not recommend pointillism (the problem of time spent with results reaped), this style has given *Miss Milo* the look of being from another time and place.